Frog is Sad

Max Velthuijs

Andersen Press • London

Copyright © 2003 by Max Velthuijs

The rights of Max Velthuijs to be identified as the author and illustrator of this work
have been asserted by him in accordance with the Copyright, Designs and Patents Act, 1988.

First published in Great Britain in 2003 by Andersen Press Ltd., 20 Vauxhall Bridge Road, London SW1V 2SA.

Published in Australia by Random House Australia Pty., 20 Alfred Street, Milsons Point, Sydney, NSW 2061.

All rights reserved. Colour separated in Switzerland by Photolitho AG, Offsetreproduktionen,
Gossau, Zürich. Printed and bound in Italy by Grafiche AZ, Verona.

10   9   8   7   6   5   4   3   2   1

British Library Cataloguing in Publication Data available.

ISBN 1 84270 289 0

This book has been printed on acid-free paper

Frog woke up feeling sad . . .

. . . he felt like crying, but he didn't know why.

Little Bear was worried. He wanted Frog to be happy.
"Please smile, Frog," he said.
"I can't," said Frog.
"But you could *yesterday*," said Little Bear.

But Frog couldn't smile today.
And he couldn't be happy.
And he wanted to be on his own.
So Little Bear went away.

Rat came by. "Cheer up, Frog!" he said.

"I can't," said Frog.

"But it's such a beautiful day!" said Rat. "You're not sick, are you?"

"No," said Frog. "I'm not sick. I'm just sad."

"Shall I make you laugh?" said Rat.
And he began to dance madly about.
But it didn't make Frog laugh.

Then, Rat walked on his hands . . .
but it didn't cheer Frog up.

Then he balanced a ball on his nose,
just like in the circus!

Frog didn't even smile.

Rat was disappointed. He didn't know what else to do.
And then he had an idea . . .

He rushed off to fetch his violin . . .

. . . and he started to play a beautiful tune,
a tune so beautiful that Frog began to cry.
He cried until the tears streamed down his cheeks.

And the more Rat played his violin, the harder Frog cried.
"But Frog, why are you crying?" asked Rat.
"Because you play so beautifully," wept Frog.
He was overcome with emotion.

At that, Rat burst out laughing.
"Oh, you are *silly*, Frog," he said. He laughed and laughed.
Frog just stood there . . .

Then, suddenly, he began to smile.
His smile grew and grew . . .

. . . until he was laughing and singing and dancing with Rat, all his sadness gone.

They made such a happy noise that Duck came running . . .

. . . and Pig and Hare . . .

. . . and Little Bear last of all.
They all fell about, roaring with laughter together.

"Oh!" gasped Frog. "I have never laughed so much
in my whole life, ever!"

"Dear Frog," said Little Bear. "I'm so glad you can
smile again. But why were you so sad in the first place?"
"I don't know," said Frog. "I just was."